PANIC IN THE CITY

The 1888 New York City Blizzard

Bonnie Highsmith Taylor

Perfection Learning®

Illustration: Margaret Sanfilippo

About the Author

Bonnie Highsmith Taylor is a native Oregonian. She loves camping in the Oregon mountains and watching birds and other wildlife. Writing is Ms. Taylor's first love. But she also enjoys going to plays and concerts, collecting antique dolls, and listening to good music.

Ms. Taylor is the author of several Chapter 2 books, including *Terror in the City: The 1906 San Francisco Earthquake* and *Valley of Disaster: The Johnstown Flood of 1889*. She has also written novels, including *Gypsy in the Cellar* and *Kodi's Mare*.

Image credits: ArtToday (www.arttoday.com) pp. 16, 36, 39, 41, 50; NOAA cover, pp. 3, 53, 59, 61, 62

For information, contact
Perfection Learning® Corporation
1000 North Second Avenue, P.O. Box 500
Logan, Iowa 51546-0500.
Phone: 1-800-831-4190 • Fax: 1-800-543-2745
perfectionlearning.com

PB ISBN-13: 978-0-7891-5557-3 ISBN-10: 0-7891-5557-5
RLB ISBN-13: 978-0-7569-0646-7 ISBN-10: 0-7569-0646-6
13 14 15 16 17 PP 20 19 18 17

TABLE OF CONTENTS

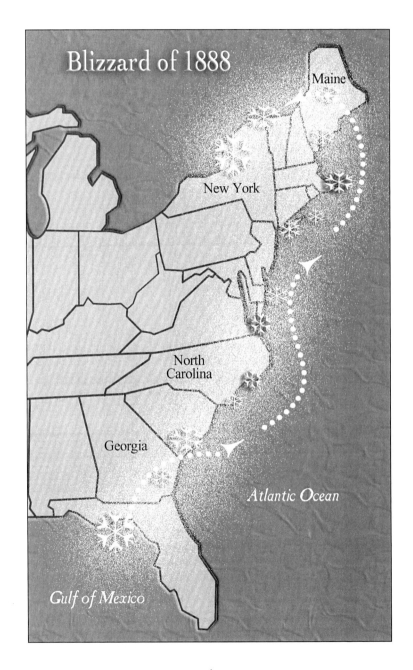

Blizzard of 1888

Maine

New York

North
Carolina

Georgia

Atlantic Ocean

Gulf of Mexico

CHAPTER 1

Gerald woke to the sound of his little sister's coughing. Her cough was getting worse.

Gerald raised up on his narrow cot.

PANIC IN THE SNOW

Six-year-old Molly slept in the bed across the room. Four-year-old Nora slept with her.

Molly's coughing had kept Gerald awake most of the night. Mama had not even gone to bed. Each time Gerald woke up in the night, he saw Mama sitting on the girls' bed. She would be giving Molly honey in warm tea. Or she would be **sponging** Molly with a damp cloth.

Molly had had the bad cough and fever for two days.

Now Mama was in the other room. The light from the **kerosene** lamp shone under the curtain covering the bedroom doorway. Gerald could hear Mama stirring the fire in the cookstove.

Gerald lay back down. He closed his eyes. He wanted so much to go back to sleep. But he felt guilty knowing that Mama had been awake all night.

Gerald sat up in bed. He pulled back the window curtain and looked out the second-story window. Daylight was just breaking. He hoped it would be warm again. The past few days, it had been unusually warm for March.

It was Sunday. The Nolan family always went to early **mass**. But Gerald knew they would not be going this morning—not with Molly sick.

Gerald looked at his sister. She was sleeping. But she was breathing heavily.

Gerald slipped out of bed and went into the kitchen. He stood by the stove in his nightshirt.

"*Brrr*," he shivered. He held his hands over the stove.

"I'll pour you some tea," Mama said. "That will warm you."

She poured Gerald a mug of hot tea. She added a spoonful of sugar and stirred it. Gerald warmed his hands on the mug as he sipped the tea.

Mama sat down at the table with her own mug of tea. Gerald could see how tired she was. Dark shadows formed under her eyes.

"Molly's real sick, isn't she?" Gerald asked.

Mama nodded. "She hasn't been well since you three children had **measles** this winter."

Gerald remembered how awful that was. They had been so sick. Poor Mama had nearly worked herself to death taking care of them.

Papa had been home then. He'd helped care for them when he could. He'd even slept in the bedroom with Gerald. The girls had slept in the other room with Mama.

PANIC IN THE SNOW

The Nolan's second-story **flat** had two rooms. Gerald slept on a cot in the bedroom. The girls slept together in the bed in the same room.

Mama and Papa slept in the big sofa bed in the other room. That room was the kitchen/living room. The flat didn't have hot water. Water had to be heated on the cookstove.

On Saturday nights, the Nolans took baths in a big tub on the kitchen floor. Mama had to heat a lot of water then.

Each floor of the building had a room with a toilet. The toilet was shared by four families.

"I wish your papa were here," said Mrs. Nolan. "I feel so lost without him."

"Me too," said Gerald. "I miss him. I can hardly wait till he gets home."

Mr. Nolan had been gone for more than a week. Papa's brother had written the Nolans about a farm next to his. It was near the town of Buffalo. The farm was for sale—cheap.

Papa had gone all the way to Buffalo on a train to see about buying the farm.

Yesterday, a letter had come from Papa. He had seen the farm and liked it. The owner had told Papa he could **sharecrop** for the first year. After that, Papa could make payments when he sold his crops.

"Can I read Papa's letter again?" Gerald asked.

Mama took the letter from a drawer and handed it to her son.

"Papa says we can have some sheep," Gerald said. "And a cow and chickens." He smiled at Mama. "You'd like that, wouldn't you?" he asked.

"Oh, yes," Mama answered. "Your

PANIC IN THE SNOW

Papa wasn't meant to live in a city. He's a farmer. Like his father and his grandfather before him. All the Nolans were farmers. Even after the potato **famine** in Ireland, they still farmed. But many of their friends and neighbors gave up their farms. They moved away. Most came to America."

At one time, potatoes were as necessary to the people of Ireland as rice was to the people of China. In 1846, the potato crops were hit by a disease. This caused a widespread famine. A million people died. Many died from starvation, and many more died from **typhus** and other diseases brought on by the famine.

More than a million people left Ireland to keep from starving. Most **emigrated** to America.

In 1845, the population of Ireland was 8,500,000. By 1851, the population had dropped to 6,500,000.

Mama sighed. "Sometimes I miss the old country," she said. "Maybe someday we can all go back for a visit."

Mama had often talked about going to Ireland for a visit. Gerald had grandparents and other relatives living there that he had never met. But he knew it would cost a lot of money for such a trip.

Gerald finished reading the letter. "Papa says the farmhouse needs some work," he said. "But it's bigger than our flat. And it has a fireplace."

"I'll miss this little flat," Mama said. "Your papa and I were newlyweds when we came to America. You were born a year later." She pointed to the sofa bed. "Right in that old sofa bed."

Gerald laughed.

Sounds of loud coughing came from the bedroom. Mama ran to Molly.

Gerald folded Papa's letter and put it back in the drawer.

CHAPTER 2

Later that morning, Mama sat
down next to Gerald. She said,
"Please go down to Mrs. Riley's and
ask her to call Dr. Duffy."

Mrs. Riley was the landlady. The Rileys were the only people on the block with a telephone.

When Gerald got back, he helped clean the flat. Mama sat by Molly until she fell asleep.

Gerald read to Nora to keep her quiet. Gerald loved to read. He checked out books from the library every Saturday.

"I wish Dr. Duffy would hurry," Mama complained. "It's almost noon. It's been nearly four hours since Mrs. Riley called him."

"Dr. Duffy told Mrs. Riley he'd get here as soon as he could," Gerald said. "He said he had lots of house calls to make."

Molly slept between coughing spells. Mama said her fever was higher. She sponged Molly several times.

At last, Dr. Duffy arrived. He took

Molly's temperature and listened to her chest.

Gerald didn't hear what the doctor said to Mama. The boy just sat patiently at the table in the other room. Nora was napping on Gerald's cot.

Finally, the doctor and Mama left the bedroom. Dr. Duffy handed Mama a bottle. "I don't have much medicine with me," he said. "But I'll write a **prescription** for more. There's enough here for today and tonight."

Gerald saw Mama's hand tremble when she took the prescription from the doctor. "Is—is she going to—to be all right, doctor?" she stammered.

Dr. Duffy patted Mama's arm. "I believe so, Mrs. Nolan. Keep her quiet. And have her drink lots of fluids. I'll check back on Tuesday."

Molly went to sleep after taking the medicine.

PANIC IN THE SNOW

"Mama," said Gerald. "You lie down and rest while the girls are sleeping. I'll go outside for a while."

Some of Gerald's friends were playing stickball in the street. Gerald joined them.

One of the boys, Luigi, was new to the neighborhood. He and his family were new to America. They had arrived from Italy only a month before. Luigi was in Gerald's sixth-grade class. Gerald was helping Luigi with his English.

Many children did not own baseballs and bats. They used heavy sticks, such as broomsticks, for bats. Balls were made from anything they could find. Bases were garbage can lids, cardboard from boxes, or lampposts.

The boys played hard. But Gerald looked up at his window often to see if Mama was calling him.

After a while, Luigi went home. He was cold.

"*Addio*," called Gerald.

Luigi grinned. "Good-bye," he answered.

Gerald and two other boys played a while longer. It began to rain a little.

"Let's go to Kepler's for candy," said Frank.

"I don't have any money," said Gerald.

"Me neither," said Leo.

Frank took a coin from his pocket. "I have a three-cent piece," he said.

> Three-cent pieces were coins used in the United States from 1851–1889.

The boys went to the little neighborhood store. They looked at all the candies. Chocolate drops, peppermint sticks, licorice, all-day suckers, and peanut brittle filled the glass jars.

Frank chose licorice. Leo chose a big all-day sucker. Gerald chose five chocolate drops. He'd take two home for his sisters.

Frank handed Mr. Kepler his three-cent piece. Gerald and Leo thanked Frank.

When they got back outside, it was raining harder. The boys decided to go home.

Gerald ran into the building. He could hear Molly coughing before he got to the second floor.

On the second-floor landing, he met Mr. O'Brian. Mr. O'Brian lived on the third floor. He delivered coal in the neighborhood.

"I'm sorry to hear that your sister is sick," said Mr. O'Brian. "I have a little bit of extra coal. I'll bring it up later. She must be kept warm."

Gerald thanked him and went into the flat.

CHAPTER 3

"Gerald, you're soaked," Mama scolded. "Do you want to be down in bed like Molly?"

Gerald took off his coat and hung it over the back of a chair. Mama handed him a towel to dry his hair.

Gerald gave Nora a chocolate drop. He put the other one in a cup on a shelf. "This is for Molly," he said. "When she gets better."

Mama looked so tired.

"I hope it stops raining," said Gerald. "When it does, I'll take Nora outside to play. Then you can get some rest."

But it didn't stop raining. It rained harder and harder. The temperature dropped. The wind began to blow.

Mr. O'Brian brought the coal. He also brought a pot of chicken soup that Mrs. O'Brian had made.

Mama thanked him and fixed him a cup of tea.

"It feels like winter is starting all over," Mr. O'Brian stated. "The last few days, it was like spring. Now it's cold again."

They talked about Mr. Nolan going to Buffalo to see about buying a farm.

"I wish you good luck," Mr. O'Brian said. "But we'll miss you a lot."

Mama and Papa had known the O'Brians a long time. They all had come to America together.

Molly slept quietly for a little over an hour. Mama lay on Gerald's cot and napped. Gerald sat at the table with his little sister. He drew funny pictures for her. They made her laugh.

✳ ✳ ✳

Mama heated up the pot of chicken soup for supper. It was so good! The family also had canned peaches with canned milk. Mama got Molly to eat a little bit of the soup.

"She didn't eat much," Mama said. "But a little bit is better than nothing. She has to keep up her strength."

Mama put the rest of the soup in the icebox for the next day.

Mama sponged Molly and gave her more medicine. Molly fell asleep. But she still coughed a lot.

That night, it got dark earlier than usual. Mama lit the kerosene lantern.

Nora was restless. She had had to be so still for the last few days.

"Play with me," she begged her brother. "Ride me piggyback."

"We have to be quiet so we don't wake Molly," Gerald explained. "She's very sick."

Gerald had read all the stories in Nora's storybook at least three times. He had used up all the paper drawing pictures for her.

"I know!" exclaimed Nora. "Let's play mountain climbing."

Mountain climbing was a game Nora and Molly played on rainy days. They climbed up and down the three flights of stairs pretending they were climbing mountains.

For 30 minutes, Gerald climbed up and down the stairs with his little sister. He wondered if she would ever get tired.

At last, Nora panted, "I—I'm tired. And thirsty."

They went back to their flat. Mama was making up the sofa bed.

"I'll try sleeping in here tonight," she said. "Nora can sleep with me. Maybe Molly will sleep better alone."

Nora was already snuggling under the covers. She was still dressed.

The wind was blowing very hard. It rattled the windows. The rain beat against the glass.

"Such a storm!" said Mama. "And it's getting so cold. We must not run out of coal. Not with Molly so sick."

Gerald agreed. He'd get more coal from Mr. O'Brian. He would offer to work for him to pay for it.

Mama shut the **damper** on the stove. "Let's go to bed early," she said. "We could all do with a good rest."

CHAPTER 4

Gerald couldn't sleep. He could hear Mama snoring. At least she was getting some sleep.

PANIC IN THE SNOW

Molly groaned a lot. But she seemed
to be coughing less. Once Gerald heard
Molly whisper "Papa" in her sleep.

Gerald tossed and turned. He tried
hard to go to sleep.

The window near his bed rattled
noisily. It sounded like little rocks hitting
the window.

Gerald raised up in bed. He pulled
back the window curtain and looked out.
Sleet was hitting the window. It was so
noisy. He hoped it wouldn't disturb Molly.

Gerald put his face close to the
window. He could see a wagon moving
slowly along the cobblestone street. The
horse was tossing its head. Sleet was
hitting it in the face. He saw the horse
slip and almost fall.

Gerald saw people walking in the
glow of the corner **gaslight**. They were
moving slowly. He saw a man slide
across the icy sidewalk. The man fell
down hard.

Just then, Officer Regan came down the street. He was slipping and sliding. The officer helped the man to his feet.

A garbage can rolled down the street. Garbage flew in all directions. Another person slipped and fell.

For a long time, Gerald watched out the window. He saw **debris** flying through the air. He saw horses rearing. He heard their loud whinnies. Gerald felt sorry for the poor animals. He knew they must be very frightened.

Molly groaned again in her sleep. Gerald turned from the window. He saw that her blanket had fallen to the floor. Gerald got up and put the blanket back over his sister. He touched her forehead. It was so hot.

He wished more and more that Papa was here. He always felt better when the family was together.

Gerald stroked Molly's head. "Go to sleep," he murmured. "Go to sleep."

He didn't want Mama to wake up. At last, Molly grew quiet.

Gerald went back to his cot. He tried not to think about the storm raging outside. The sound of the wind grew louder. The window rattled hard.

Gerald thought about Papa far away in Buffalo. He wondered what it would be like to live on a farm. Gerald had never even seen a farm.

Gerald had seen a lot of horses. But he had seen only pictures of other farm animals. He had never seen cows, pigs, sheep, or even chickens.

Maybe I can have a dog, Gerald thought. And the girls can have a cat.

Mama had said they would have all the milk, butter, and eggs they wanted. Living on a farm might be nice, Gerald thought.

But he would miss the city. He would miss all of his friends and his school. He would miss the excitement of the busy streets. And he would miss the cozy flat where he and his little sisters had been born—the flat where Mama and Papa had lived since they came to America.

At last, Gerald slept.

CHAPTER 5

Molly's coughing woke Gerald with a start. She was choking.

Mama came running. She carried the medicine Dr. Duffy had given her. She had to wait for Molly to quit coughing.

Gerald watched Mama give Molly the last of the medicine. He went into the other room. Nora was fast asleep. Gerald put on his clothes. He stirred the fire and added a hunk of coal.

In a few moments, Mama came out of the bedroom. She had dressed. She carried the empty bottle. "Her medicine is all gone," Mama said.

"Is she any better?" asked Gerald.

"She's not quite as hot," Mama said. "But her cough is so bad. She needs more medicine."

"I'll go to the drugstore," Gerald said. "I'll get the prescription filled."

Mama raised the blind. "Oh,

my!" she exclaimed.

Gerald went to the window. He couldn't believe it. Snow was falling so hard that he could not see the street. He had never seen such large flakes. The snow swirled in all directions. The wind was blowing harder than ever.

"You can't go out in this, Gerald," Mama said. "It would be too dangerous."

Gerald didn't answer. He was thinking hard. How could he get to the drugstore? It was only four blocks away.

Gerald had warm clothes. He had woolen gloves, a stocking cap, and a scarf. He didn't have any boots. But he did have high-top shoes.

"I'm going downstairs, Mama," Gerald said. " I want to see how deep the snow is."

It was all Gerald could do to open the big front door in the hallway. Snow blew inside. The wind nearly whipped the door out of his hands.

The snow was very deep. Some of the drifts were almost as tall as Gerald.

It must have snowed all night, Gerald thought.

Gerald closed the door. He went back to his flat. Mama had hot cereal and toast ready.

Nora was awake and sitting at the table. Mama and Gerald joined her. They ate in silence.

Gerald thought hard. He had to find some way to get to the drugstore. Molly needed the medicine.

"If only I had some snowshoes," Gerald thought out loud. "I could get through the snow."

"Snowshoes?" Nora said. "Shoes made out of snow?"

Mama and Gerald laughed.

"No, Nora," Gerald said. "Things to put on your feet. Then you can walk on top of the snow. I read about them in school. Eskimos who live in the far north use snowshoes."

"But you don't have any," Nora said.

Gerald thought and thought. "If I had something to make snowshoes with—"

Suddenly, an idea came to him. "I'll be right back," he called as he rushed out the door.

In the basement, Gerald found what he was looking for. He grabbed a saw and cut the handles off two old straw brooms. Then he carried the broom heads and some wire upstairs.

"My land," Mama said. "What have you got?"

"Snowshoes," Gerald grinned.

Snowshoes look like long, oval tennis rackets. They are usually about three feet long. They help a person walk on deep snow without sinking.

Snowshoes were first made and used by North American Indians. White hunters, trappers, and farmers used them too.

The frames were made of light wood that was easy to bend. Long strips of animal skins were stretched over the frames.

Eskimos were experts on snowshoes. They could walk for hours at up to six miles per hour. They could run at ten miles per hour.

Today, most snowshoes have light metal frames. In some places, snowshoe clubs have formed. The members have snowshoe races.

Mama and Nora watched. Gerald ran long pieces of wire through the broom straws. He placed his feet on the broom heads. He wrapped the wire around his shoes tightly.

Then he stood up and walked clumsily around the room. Nora giggled.

"I think it will work, Mama," Gerald said. "I'm going after the medicine."

Mama gave him the money and the prescription. "I don't like this, Gerald," she said. "I don't like it at all. This is a very bad storm."

"It's only four blocks, Mama. I can make it," Gerald said.

He put on his heavy coat. Then he pulled on his gloves, cap, and scarf.

It was awkward going down the stairs. And it was hard opening the heavy front door.

At last, Gerald was on the sidewalk. A strong gust of wind hit him instantly. His scarf whipped from around his neck. It sailed through the air.

Gerald pulled his cap down over his ears. He turned up his coat collar.

The wind was so strong and cold. It was all Gerald could do to push himself against the wind. His feet felt very heavy.

On Gerald plodded. He could hardly keep his eyes open. The wind hit him with so much force that it stung his skin.

Gerald was surprised to see so many people. Mostly, they were men and women. He saw very few children.

Surely, he thought, school is closed today.

Overhead, wires were snapping and falling down. Windows were shattering. Horses whinnied with fear.

PANIC IN THE SNOW

People screamed as debris flew through the air and struck them.

Just ahead, Gerald saw a store awning break loose. A young woman was walking under it.

Before the blizzard, hundreds of telegraph, electric, and telephone wires lined the streets of New York City. Nearly every wire fell during the storm. After the blizzard, utility wires were buried underground.

PANIC IN THE SNOW

"Look out!" Gerald shouted.

But the woman didn't hear. The awning's metal frame hit her on the head. She cried out as she fell.

It took Gerald several moments to reach her. He discovered it was Mary Dugan. She lived in the building next to Gerald. Mary was only 14.

> Many children held full-time jobs. At the age of 13, they could work in factories. Younger children earned money by making **artificial** flowers, delivering groceries, and selling newspapers. Western Union hired boys from age 12 to 14 as messengers.

At last, Gerald was able to free Mary. She had a large bump on her forehead. She was crying.

"I must get to work," she sobbed. "I can't lose my job."

Before Gerald could answer, Officer Murray was there.

PANIC IN THE SNOW

"There now, miss," the officer said. "I'll take you home. No doubt the plant will be closed today anyway. Most of the **els** are stranded."

The elevated railroads were fairly new in 1888. They were high in the air—about as high as the second story of most buildings. They were supposed to be blizzard-proof. But they became stalled even before all other traffic.

The train stations were reached by climbing tall iron stairways.

The elevated trains were in use for over 60 years. In 1900, the building of the New York subway system began. The subway replaced the els.

"But I can't stay home because of the snow," Mary sniffled.

"Miss, this is much more than just snow," replied Officer Murray. "This is a bad blizzard. Probably the worst blizzard to hit this part of the country."

Finally, Mary gave in. But she was still sobbing. Officer Murray took her arm and led her home.

"You be careful, young man," he called to Gerald. "Don't go too far from home."

Gerald didn't take time to tell the officer where he was going. He started on his way. He had only two more blocks to go. Then he would get Molly's medicine and go home.

Twice, Gerald stopped to help someone stuck in a snowdrift. He even saw a man actually picked up by the wind. He landed head first in the snow.

PANIC IN THE SNOW

At last, Gerald reached McPherson's drugstore.

But—the drugstore was closed!

CHAPTER 6

Gerald's spirits sank. He rattled the door of the drugstore. But no one answered.

PANIC IN THE SNOW

What was he going to do? Molly had to have the medicine. Mama was counting on him. He must be the man of the family while Papa was gone.

Many people stopped and stared when they saw Gerald's straw snowshoes. Some of them laughed. But many of them told him what a bright idea he had come up with.

Gerald beamed when one man said, "When you get ready to go to work, son, come and see me." He handed Gerald a business card. "I could use a bright young man like you," he said.

Gerald read the card. The man was the owner of a company that made umbrellas.

The snow was falling even harder. Gerald could hardly stand up against the wind. But he knew he couldn't go home without Molly's medicine.

A man was struggling by in the snow.

"Could you tell me where another drugstore is?" Gerald asked.

"There's one on Third Avenue," the man answered. "But that's a long walk. It's dangerous being out in this weather."

Gerald thanked the man. He started toward Third Avenue.

Gerald had no idea how long it would take him. He only knew that his little sister needed the medicine.

The boy trudged along slowly. His legs ached. His face stung from the icy snow. He covered his face with one hand. When he looked at his glove, he saw blood on it. His face was bleeding from the freezing snow hitting it.

When Gerald got to 48th Street, he saw an el stopped on the track. Snow was over the top of the wheels.

Gerald could barely see passengers through the windows. But he could tell they were panicking. Some were pushing other people.

Gerald was glad he was not on the train. It would be frightening to be stranded up so high. There was no way to get down.

But then, Gerald saw people heading toward the stalled train. Some were carrying ladders.

Gerald heard a young man shouting, "Ten cents each for use of my ladder! Ten cents!"

People were scrambling out of the train. They were shouting and shoving one another.

Gerald watched for a few moments. His legs were growing numb. He could hardly move his fingers. His ears were tingling. He knew he shouldn't stop for long.

Gerald hurried on as fast as he could. His broom snowshoes were awkward. But they kept him from sinking in the snow.

* * *

It was over 30 minutes before he reached the drugstore on Third Avenue. No one was in the store except the druggist.

Gerald was breathing hard. He could barely feel his hands and feet. He stumbled toward the big coal heating stove in the corner.

"Don't get warm too fast," the druggist said.

Gerald handed him the prescription. "My—my sister is—is very sick," Gerald whispered. His throat hurt when he talked.

"I'll get this filled right away," the druggist said. "You sit down and rest a bit."

Gerald plopped down on a bench. He tried to wiggle his toes. They hurt.

"Those are some snowshoes you've got there," the druggist said.

Gerald tried to smile. But he couldn't do it. His face felt numb.

Gerald began to grow sleepy. He had heard that people who freeze to death simply fall asleep.

The boy staggered to his feet. He forced himself to walk around the store.

The druggist gave Gerald the medicine. "You be careful going home, young man," he said. "And I hope your sister gets better."

Gerald thanked the man and left.

The wind and cold were worse than ever. Gerald wondered if he would make it. He hurt so bad. And he was so tired and sleepy.

PANIC IN THE SNOW

In the middle of the street, a wagon was half buried in the snow. The horse, still in **harness**, was dead. It had frozen to death.

Many animals suffered during the blizzard. Horses froze to death while still harnessed. Hundreds of frozen birds, usually sparrows, fell dead from their perches onto the sidewalks.

Gerald's stomach lurched. He swallowed hard. But on he trudged. He could barely raise his feet.

Gerald thought about Papa. He wondered if it was storming where he was.

Gerald tried to keep from thinking about how cold he was. He thought about summer. He thought about going barefoot and burning his feet on the hot pavement. He thought about swimming in the ocean.

But Gerald was so miserable. He felt like crying.

Suddenly, Gerald heard a voice over the roaring of the wind. He turned his head. It was Officer Murray.

"Are you still out in this storm, young fellow?" He took Gerald's arm. "I'll walk home with you. You're just about ready to drop."

Gerald was happy for the company. Officer Murray had to yell to be heard.

He told Gerald that the storm had caused a lot of injuries. Most of them were frostbitten ears and fingers. Some people were injured by flying debris. The storm had caused some deaths to humans and animals.

The officer walked Gerald all the way to his apartment building.

"Do you need help up the stairs?" Officer Murray asked Gerald.

"N—no, s—sir," Gerald answered through chattering teeth. "I'll be fine. Thank—thank you so m—much."

Minutes later, Gerald was in his warm home. He was eating a bowl of chicken soup. Mama had nearly hugged the breath out of him.

"Oh, I was so worried," Mama had said over and over. "I didn't know what had happened."

Nora hugged her brother too. "I was worried too," she said.

How good it was to be home. How good it was to be with his family. But the best thing of all happened a few days later when Papa came home.

"I'm really proud of you, son," Papa said. "You did a good job as man of the house."

AFTERWORD

The blizzard of 1888 was called "The Great White Hurricane." A snowstorm is called a *blizzard* when the wind blows more than 35 miles per hour and **visibility** is less than 500 feet.

In severe blizzards, winds reach 45 miles per hour or more. Temperatures can be 10°F or lower.

During the 1888 blizzard in New York City, wind gusts exceeded 70 miles per hour. Twenty-two inches of snow fell. Some snowdrifts were over six feet deep. The storm lasted 36 hours.

The 1888 storm formed in the northern Gulf of Mexico on March 10. It was a weak storm system at the time.

By March 11, the storm had passed through Georgia and moved on to the North Carolina coast. As it moved north, the storm became stronger. It continued up along the East coast all the way to Maine. The main force hit New York City on March 12.

Some places received much more snow than New York City. Saratoga Springs, New York, got 50 inches of snow.

But because New York was the largest city, it was the hardest hit. Almost the entire city came to a standstill. The storm affected more people in New York City than anywhere else along its path.

In the frigid Atlantic Ocean, 200 ships were grounded or sunk. The winds at sea blew up to 90 miles per hour. About 100 seamen died. All together more than 400 people died during the storm. Most perished because of **exposure**. But some were killed by flying debris.

The United States Weather Service tower was on top of the Equitable Life Assurance Building on Broadway. The tower was 172 feet above the city streets. The weather instruments recorded the wind speed, the temperature, **precipitation**, and **humidity**. The Army Signal Corps was in charge of the weather station.

On the morning of March 12, the *anemometer*, or wind gauge, froze stiff. The only way to free it was by climbing a 25-foot pole. The pole was 4 inches in diameter.

A staff member, Sergeant Francis Long, volunteered to climb the pole. He was told that it was much too dangerous. But Sergeant Long insisted.

Sergeant Long climbed the pole and freed the gauge. Using one hand, he also replaced some broken wiring. It was all he could do to hold on in the strong wind.

Sergeant Long's hands were nearly frozen. But because of his efforts, the Weather Bureau was able to record the information of America's most famous blizzard.

Most everything in New York City was closed during the blizzard. Some New Yorkers showed their sense of humor by the signs they hung in their windows before closing.

In front of a closed flower shop was a sign that said

> **Don't Pick**
> **the**
> **Flowers.**

Other signs read

In some cases, business went on as usual. Barnum and Bailey Circus put on its scheduled performance on Monday afternoon, March 12. About 100 people showed up. Phineas T. Barnum told the audience, "The storm may be a great show, but I still have the Greatest Show on Earth!"

Three Broadway theaters gave performances. At one, four people sat in the audience. Most of the show's performers and musicians did not show up. But five orchestra members and three performers put on the entire show.

In 1929, the Society of Blizzard Men was started. Men who had lived through the storm gathered together every March 12 for a luncheon. Later, the Society of Blizzard Women was organized.

Other Blizzards of Record

* Armistice Day Storm
    November 11–12, 1940

* The Great Midwest Blizzard
    January 26–27, 1967

* Blizzard of 1978
    January 25–27, 1978

* Storm of the Century
    March 13–14, 1993

* Blizzard of 1996
    January 7–8, 1996

GLOSSARY

artificial   fake but resembling
                    the real thing

....

damper   plate in a chimney
                    that controls the air
                    flow

debris rubbish that remains after something is destroyed

....

el shortened form for *elevated train*. It runs on tracks above the street level.

....

emigrate to leave one's home to live somewhere else

....

exposure condition of being unprotected in severe weather

....

famine extreme shortage of food

flat apartment

gaslight lamp that burns gas
for its energy
source

harness   set of straps for a
horse to which a
wagon or buggy is
attached

humidity   amount of
moisture in the air

kerosene   fuel oil

mass church service
....

measles contagious disease
caused by a virus
....

precipitation hail, mist, rain,
sleet, or snow that
falls to the ground
....

prescription written instructions
for the preparation
and the use of
medicine
....

sharecrop to farm land as a
renter and receive
part of the profits
....

sponge to wipe the body
with a damp cloth
to bring down a
fever

typhus	severe disease that causes high fever, headache, and a dark red rash
visibility	distance one can see